THE STORY OF A MONKEY ON A STICK

LAURA LEE HOPE

THE STORY OF A MONKEY ON A STICK

CHAPTER I

A STRANGE AWAKENING

The Monkey on a Stick opened his eyes and looked around. That is he tried to look around; but all he could see, on all sides of him, was pasteboard box. He was lying on his back, with his hands and feet clasped around the stick, up which he had climbed so often.

"Well, this is very strange," said the Monkey on a Stick, as he rubbed his nose with one hand, "very strange indeed! Why should I wake up here, when last night I went to sleep in the toy store? I can't understand this at all!"

Once more he looked about him. He surely was inside a pasteboard box. He could see the cover of it over his head as he lay on his back, and he could see one side of the box toward his left hand, while another side of the box was at his right hand.

"And," said the Monkey on a Stick, speaking to himself, as he often did, "I suppose the bottom of the pasteboard box is under me. I must be lying on that."

He unclasped the toes of his left foot from the stick and banged his foot down two or three times.

"Yes, there's pasteboard all around me," said the Monkey. "This surely is very strange! I wonder if the Calico Clown has been up to any of his tricks? Maybe he thinks I'm a riddle, and he's going to tell it to the Elephant from the Noah's Ark, or else make a joke of me to the Jumping Jack. I haven't been shut up in a box before—not since the time Santa Claus brought me from his workshop at the North Pole. I wonder what this means?"

The Monkey raised his head and banged it on the box cover.

"Oh, my cocoanut!" cried the Monkey, for that is what he sometimes called his head. "My poor cocoanut!" he went on, as he put up his hand. "I wonder if I raised a big lump on my cocoanut!"

But his head seemed to be all right, and, taking care not to bang himself again, the Monkey began pushing on the box cover. It was not heavy, and he slowly raised it until he could look out.

As I have told you in the other books of this series, the Monkey on a Stick, and the other toys as well, could move about and talk, when they kept to certain rules. You may find out what those rules were by looking in the other books.

The Monkey on a Stick looked out from beneath the cover of the box, and what he saw surprised him almost as much as he had been startled when he found pasteboard on all sides of him. For the Monkey saw that he was in the room of a strange house, and not in the big toy department of the store where he had lived for so long a time.

"I say!" chattered the Monkey to himself, "there is something wrong here. They must have given me paregoric to make me sleep, and then have put me in a box and carted me down to some other part of the store. I'm sure the Calico Clown must have had a hand in this. He and his jokes and riddles about what makes more noise than a pig under a gate! I'll fix him when I get out of here!"

The Monkey raised the box cover higher and began to call:

"Hi there, Calico Clown! what do you mean by shutting me up in a pasteboard box? What's the joke? Come on, Mr. Elephant from Noah's Ark! Come and help me out! Ho, Jack-Jump! Hi, Jack-Box! Where are you all? I don't see any of you!"

For, as he looked around the room, from under the cover of the box, the Monkey saw not a sign of his former friends.

"This is stranger and stranger," he murmured. "I say!" he cried aloud again, "isn't any one here?"

"Yes, I'm here," answered a voice which, the Monkey knew at once, came from a toy like himself. "What's the trouble?" this voice went on. "Why are you making such a fuss? Who are you, anyhow?"

"I'm a Monkey on a Stick," answered the toy chap in the box. "And who are you? I seem to know your voice. Where are you?"

"Here I am," came the answer.

The Monkey raised the box cover higher, and then he cried:

"Why, bless my tail! The Candy Rabbit! Well, of all things! Oh, I'm so glad to see you! How are you?" and the Monkey jumped out of his box, and, laying down his stick, ran across the table and shook paws with a beautiful Candy Rabbit, who had a pink nose and pink glass eyes. The Rabbit was on the table, and the Monkey saw that his pasteboard box was there likewise.

"I am quite well, thank you," answered the Candy Rabbit, as he waved his big ears to and fro. "And I am glad to see you—very glad! I knew there was some kind of toy in that box, but I did not know it was you. I haven't seen you since we lived in the toy store together, with the Sawdust Doll, the Lamb on Wheels, the Bold Tin Soldier, the Calico Clown and the White Rocking Horse."

"Yes, and don't forget the two Jacks," went on the Monkey on a Stick, "the Jumping Jack and the Jack in the Box. Then there was the Elephant who tried to race on roller skates with the White Rocking Horse."

"I'm not forgetting them," answered the Rabbit.

"But listen!" exclaimed the Monkey. "Can you tell me this? I went to sleep in the toy store, and I woke up here—in a house, I guess it is—in a pasteboard box on a table set with dishes."

"Yes, this is a house," said the Candy Rabbit. "I live here with a little girl named Madeline. There is also a boy named Herbert here. And these really are dishes on the table. It is the breakfast table, and soon the children will be down to eat."

"But what am I doing here?" asked the Monkey in great surprise. "I can't understand it! Why am I here? I went to sleep in the store, and I woke up on a breakfast table. Can this be a trick or a riddle of the Calico Clown's? Is he going to ask what is more surprised than a Monkey on a Stick at the breakfast table, as he asks what makes more noise than a pig under a gate?"

"No, I think the Calico Clown had nothing to do with your being here," said the Candy Rabbit with a smile.

"Then who did?" asked the Monkey.

"Herbert. A boy who lives here with his sister Madeline," went on the Rabbit.

"Dear me! this is getting more and more riddly-like and jokey," said the Monkey. "I don't understand it at all! Why am I not in the store where I belong?"

"Because you don't belong there any more," cried the Candy Rabbit. "You were bought for the boy Herbert, and you are here at his breakfast plate as a surprise."

"Well, he isn't going to be any more surprised than I am," chattered the Monkey. "I don't seem to understand this at all. How did I get here?"

"I imagine that, after you went to sleep in the store last night, one of the clerks at the toy counter put you in the pasteboard box, wrapped you up and sent you here."

"I see how it happened," said the Monkey. "I went to sleep in the store yesterday afternoon. I had been up late the night before, as we toys were having some fun. I was trying to guess a riddle the Calico Clown asked. It was how do the seeds get inside the apple when there aren't any holes in the skin. I was thinking of that riddle, and it kept me up quite late the night before."

"Did you think of the answer?"

"No, I didn't," said the Monkey; "any more than I can think of the answer to the Clown's riddle of what makes more noise than a——"

"Hush! Here come Madeline and Herbert to breakfast!" suddenly whispered the Rabbit. "Back to your box as quick as you can. We toys are not allowed to move about by ourselves when any one sees us, you know."

"Yes, I know!" chattered the Monkey.

Nimbly he sprang back to his box, and clasped the stick, up and down which he climbed when a string was pulled. As he pulled the box cover down over his head he heard the joyous shouts and laughter of two children as they ran into the room.

"Happy birthday, Herbert!" called Madeline. "Look and see what Daddy bought for you yesterday!"

When Herbert had the cover off the box and had looked at the Monkey on a Stick lying there with a funny grin on his face, the boy smiled and cried:

"Oh, it's a Climbing Monkey! Oh, this is just what I wanted! Oh, now I can have a show and a circus and I'll ask Dick to come and bring his Rocking Horse, and Arnold can come and bring his Bold Tin Soldier, and we'll have lots of fun. Oh, look at my Monkey climb his stick!"

Herbert took his new birthday toy from the box, and, by pulling the string, made the Monkey go up and down as fast as anything. Madeline picked up her Candy Rabbit, and though that Bunny said nothing, he could see all that went on.

"Oh, this is a dandy Monkey!" cried Herbert. "I can give a show with him!"

While the little boy was making the funny chap go up and down the stick, the door of the breakfast room opened and some one came in.

CHAPTER II

THE MONKEY AT SCHOOL

"Well, children, why aren't you eating breakfast?" a voice asked, and Herbert, turning around, saw his mother. The Monkey on a Stick, who, if he could not talk or do any tricks just then, could use his eyes, saw a pleasant-faced lady entering the room. She was smiling at Madeline, who had her Candy Rabbit in her hands, and at Herbert.

"Oh, look, Mother, what I found at my plate!" exclaimed Herbert, and he pulled the string, and made the Monkey run up and down the stick. "It's my birthday present!"

"Yes, Daddy said he was going to get you something," said Mother. "It came from the store late yesterday afternoon, and I put it away, and had it laid at your breakfast place this morning. Do you like it?"

"Oh, it's dandy!" exclaimed Herbert. "I love it!"

The children sat down and had an orange and some oatmeal and a glass of milk and a roll with golden yellow butter on it. But of course the Monkey and the Candy Rabbit had nothing to eat. They did not want anything. Being toys, you see, they did not have to eat. Though, at times, they could eat certain things if they wished.

Madeline kept her Candy Rabbit near her plate. All of a sudden, as the little girl was eating, she dropped her spoon in her oatmeal dish, and a drop of milk spattered into the glass eye of the Candy Rabbit.

"Oh, look what you did!" exclaimed Herbert, who saw what had happened. "You'll blind your Rabbit."

"Oh, my poor Rabbit!" said Madeline, and, with her napkin, she carefully wiped the drop of milk out of the Rabbit's eye. And the Bunny never even blinked. That's what it is to be a Candy Rabbit, and have glass eyes. Not all of us are as lucky as that, are we?

A little later Herbert dropped a piece of his buttered roll. It fell near the Monkey, who was lying on the table near the breakfast plate of the little boy. Some of the butter from the roll stuck to the stick which the Monkey climbed up and down.

"Now look what you did, Herbert!" said Madeline. "You'll make the stick so slippery with butter that the Monkey may fall off."

"Come, children," called Mother, as she again entered the room. "You must finish your breakfast and go to school. Put your Monkey back in the box, Herbert. Don't be late for school."

"No'm, we won't!" promised the brother and sister.

A little later they were on their way, walking side by side on the path that led to the red school house down by the white bridge. Madeline looked at her brother curiously as they came near the building where they studied their lessons.

"Have you got your books under your coat, Herbert?" asked Madeline.

"No, I haven't my books," he said.

"Well, what have you?" asked Madeline. "You have something, for I can see a lump. What is it?"

Before Herbert could answer, if he had wanted to, the bell rang and the two children, and some others who were straggling along, had to run so they would not be late. Then, for a time, Madeline forgot what it was her brother was bringing to school under his coat.

Just before recess, his teacher, looking down toward Herbert, sitting near Dick and Arnold, called out:

"What have you there, Herbert? What are you showing to the other boys under your desk?"

"It—it's a Monkey!" answered Madeline's brother.

"A monkey!" exclaimed the teacher.

"Yes. It's my birthday Monkey," went on the little boy.

"Oh! A birthday monkey!" the teacher said again. "I think I had better call the janitor and have him take care of your monkey for you," and she started toward the door.

"Oh, no'm! He isn't a live monkey," said Herbert. "He's just a toy one, on a stick."

"Herbert, you may bring me that Monkey," the teacher said, and Herbert, very red in the face, walked up to the platform on which stood his teacher's desk. In his hand Herbert carried his Monkey on a Stick.

"Where did you get this?" his teacher asked, as she took the toy from Herbert and laid it on top of her desk.

"I got it for my birthday," he answered. "This morning."

"But why did you bring it to school?" went on the teacher. "You are nearly always a good boy. Why did you bring your Monkey to school, Herbert?"

"Oh, I—I just wanted to show him to Arnold and Dick," was the answer. "We're going to have a show, and my Monkey is going to be in it. I brought him to school under my coat!"

"Oh! Oh!" exclaimed Madeline, before she thought what she was saying. "I saw something under his coat, and I thought it was his books. Oh! Oh! And it was his Monkey!"

All the children laughed when Madeline said this, and even the teacher could not help smiling. But she said:

"Silence, please, children. We must keep on with our lessons. And, Herbert, it was wrong of you to bring your Monkey to school and take him out to show to other boys. As a little punishment I shall keep your toy in my desk until after school to-night. Then you may have him back."

"Yes'm," returned Herbert, still rather red in the face. He went back to his desk, and the other children went on with their lessons.

The teacher put the Monkey on a Stick inside a big drawer.

"Well, this is the first of my adventures since I went to sleep in the store and awakened in Herbert's house," thought the Monkey to himself, as he found that he was shut up inside the teacher's desk. "I wondered what Herbert was going to do with me when he slipped me under his coat at the breakfast table. Now I must see what we have here."

It was not very dark inside the drawer of the teacher's desk. Enough light came through the keyhole for the Monkey to see, and, among other things, he noticed a bottle of ink and a small Doll. He was pleased to see the Doll.

"Oh, here is a toy like myself!" said the Monkey, speaking in a whisper. "How do you do?" he went on, sitting up and bowing to his new acquaintance. "Are you any relation to the Sawdust Doll?" he asked politely.

"I'm a second or third cousin," was the answer. "She is stuffed with sawdust, but I am stuffed with cotton."

"Then I will call you Miss Cotton Doll," went on the Monkey. "What brought you here? Were you so bad in school that you had to be shut up in a desk?"

"No, not exactly. But a little girl named Mary brought me in her school bag yesterday, and she took me out in the study hour, and the teacher said it was wrong. So she took me away from the little girl named Mary."

"I thought Mary brought a lamb to school," said the Monkey on a Stick, who, having lived in a toy store, of course knew all about toy books and Mother Goose verses.

"That was another Mary," went on the Cotton Doll. "Besides Mary didn't bring the lamb to school, it followed her one day."

"Oh, so it did—I had forgotten," went on the Monkey.

"But my Mary brought me to school," said the Cotton Doll, "and her teacher took me away. She put me in this desk drawer; the teacher did."

"Well, now we're here, let's have some fun," said the Monkey to the Cotton Doll after a bit. "We are all alone by ourselves, and we can do as we please. Let's look around and play. We can't stand up, as the drawer isn't high enough, but we can crawl on our knees. Let's see what else is here."

"All right," agreed the Cotton Doll. So while the teacher was hearing the lessons of Herbert, Madeline and the other boys and girls, the Monkey (crawling off his stick for the time being) and the Cotton Doll went creeping on their hands and knees around the drawer.

"Let's look in the bottle of ink," proposed the Monkey, as he crawled near it, and began pulling at the cork.

"Oh, don't do that!" cried the Cotton Doll, in a whisper, of course. "Don't open it! You'll get all black!"

"Oh, if it's black ink, I know what we can do!" said the Monkey. "We can black up like colored minstrels, and have a little show in here by ourselves. I'll black your face with the ink, and you can black mine, though I am pretty brown now."

"But I don't want my face blacked with ink!" cried the Cotton Doll, as the Monkey took the cork from the bottle. "I don't want to be a minstrel!"

"Oh, but you must!" insisted the Monkey, laughing, and, catching hold of the Cotton Doll in one hand, he tilted up the ink bottle in the other, and dipped in the end of his tail.

"Now I'll paint you nice and black!" he laughed.

"Oh, don't! Please don't!" begged the Cotton Doll, as she tried to get away from the Monkey. But she couldn't, for he held her tightly, and the inky end of the tail was coming nearer and nearer to her face.

CHAPTER III

THE JANITOR'S HOUSE

"There you are! Oh, how funny you look!" chattered the Monkey on a Stick in a whisper to the Cotton Doll, as they were both shut up together in the teacher's desk. "You don't know how funny you look! If I only had a looking-glass I'd show you!"

"I don't care! I think you're real mean!" said the Cotton Doll. "Don't you dare put any more ink on me!"

"I guess I've got enough on you now!" laughed the Monkey. "There's a spot on your nose, one on your chin, and one on each of your cheeks." As he spoke the Monkey put the cork back in the ink bottle and wiped the inky end of his tail off on a piece of blotting paper in the desk.

"What's that you say?" cried the Cotton Doll. "Did you dare put ink on my nose, on my chin and my cheeks?"

"That's what I did, just for fun!" chattered the mischievous Monkey. And, really, he had done just that. Oh, he was a regular "cut-up" when he was by himself, that Monkey was.

"I must look terrible!" said the poor Cotton Doll, and, raising her hands, she rubbed them over her face. She felt the wet spots where the Monkey had daubed her with ink.

"Oh! aren't you mean?" cried the Cotton Doll. "My little girl mistress will never like me again when the teacher gives me back to her. I'm all spoiled!"

"No, you just look funny!" laughed the Monkey. "You looked funny when I put ink spots on you, but now you look funnier than ever, 'cause you've spread the ink all around, and made big splotches of it. Oh, my! Excuse me while I laugh!" he cried, and he wiggled and twisted around on the bottom of the drawer, laughing in whispers at the funny look on the face of the Cotton Doll.

"You're too mean for anything!" said the Doll to the Monkey, and she was almost ready to cry. But she happened to think that if she shed any tears they would wash down through the ink on her cheeks and make her look queerer than ever. So she did not cry.

"I'm never going to speak to you again, so there!" exclaimed the Cotton Doll, and she would have stamped her foot if there had been room for her to stand up in the desk drawer—which there wasn't. So she just banged her heels on the bottom of it.

"Oh, I'll be good!" promised the Monkey. "I won't put any more ink on you, and I'll see if I can get some of it off on this piece of blotting paper. I blotted my tail on it."

He tried to clean the Doll's face, but, by this time, the ink had dried, and you know how hard it is to get dried ink off your fingers after you have written a letter. Well, it was this way with the Cotton Doll. The ink stayed on her face.

"Well, if you have ink on your face I've also got some on the end of my tail, where I dipped it into the bottle," said the Monkey chap, thinking to cheer up the Doll by this.

"Yes, but the ink doesn't show on your brown tail as it does on my white face," said the Doll. "However, there is no use crying over spilled milk, I suppose," she went on. "Only if you do such a thing again I'll never speak to you as long as I live!"

"I'll never do it again," said the Monkey in a sorrowful voice. "Now let's have some fun. You tell me some of your adventures and I'll tell you some of mine. Did you ever live in a store?"

"Oh, yes, that's where I came from," answered the Doll.

"And was there a Calico Clown in your store, who was always asking what it was that made more noise than a pig under a gate?" asked the Monkey.

"No. But there was a Jumping Jack who was always trying to see how high he could kick, and one day he nearly kicked my hat off," said the Cotton Doll. "But tell me, please, some of your adventures."

The Monkey was just starting to tell how the Calico Clown's red and yellow trousers were burned in the gas jet one day, when, all of a sudden, there was a great noise and commotion in the schoolroom. The Monkey and the Doll could not tell what had caused it, though the Monkey did try to look out through the keyhole.

"Can you see anything?" asked the Doll.

"I can see some water dripping down," answered the long-tailed chap, "and the teacher and the children are running around as fast as anything."

"Oh, I wonder what has happened!" exclaimed the Doll. And just then she and the Monkey on a Stick heard the teacher say:

"Run out quickly, children! Run out, all of you. A water pipe has burst and there's a regular rain storm inside our nice schoolroom."

"Please can't I have my Monkey on a Stick before I go out?" asked Herbert. "You put him in your desk, Teacher!"

"And I want my knife you took away, please!" called another boy.

"We have no time for those things, now," the teacher said. "The water is coming down fast, and we'll all be wet through if we stay. The Monkey, knife and other things will be all right in my desk. Get your hats, and pass out quickly. More pipes may burst and flood the school.

"Go home, children, all of you," said the teacher. "To-morrow the pipes will be mended, and, if the school is dry enough, we will go on with our lessons. But run home now."

You may well imagine that most of the boys and girls were glad of the holiday that had come to them so unexpectedly. But Herbert felt sorry; that he had to leave his Monkey on a Stick in school. When he reached home he acted so strangely that his mother wanted to know what the matter was.

Of course Herbert had to tell that he had taken his Monkey to school, and he also had to tell what had happened afterward.

"Of course you did wrong," said Herbert's mother, "and you must suffer a little punishment."

"What kind of punishment?" asked Herbert.

"The punishment of not having your Monkey," was the answer.

And now we must see what happened to the Monkey on a Stick.

"What do you imagine will happen next?" asked the Doll of the Monkey, for they had heard what had been said.

"I don't know," was the answer. "But if we are left alone here in the room we can get out of the desk and have some fun."

"Oh, so we can!" cried the Doll. "I'm tired of being shut up here. Can you open the desk, Mr. Monkey?"

"I think so," was the reply.

The Monkey was just going to raise the lid, by prying under it with the long stick up and down which he climbed, when, all of a sudden, there was a noise in the room.

"Some one is coming!" whispered the Doll.

"I hear them," said the Monkey. He looked out through the keyhole and saw a man wading through the water toward the desk. "I guess it's the night watchman," went on the Monkey in a whisper.

"We don't have a night watchman in school," whispered back the Doll. "But we have a janitor. Maybe it's the janitor coming."

And so it was. The janitor had shut off some of the water in the broken pipes, and he was going about from room to room to see how much damage had been done. He walked up to the desk inside of which the Monkey and Doll had been placed.

"Well, I do declare!" exclaimed the janitor, and the Monkey and the Doll heard him. "There's ink running out of the drawer of the teacher's desk! Ink running out of her desk, and water running out of the broken pipes! Sure the school had bad luck to-day! But I must see about this ink. It may spoil everything in the drawer. The bottle must have been upset and the cork came out when the teacher and children were running around after the pipes burst."

The Monkey turned away from the keyhole and looked at the bottle of ink. Surely enough, it lay on its side, and the cork was out. A stream of black liquid was running out of the bottle, dripping down through a crack in the teacher's desk.

"Oh, do you suppose you did that?" asked the Doll in a whisper of the Monkey.

"I—I guess maybe I did," he answered. "After I dipped my tail in the ink and marked your face, maybe I didn't put the cork back in tightly enough. And when I jumped around, to see what all the racket was about, I must have knocked the bottle over."

The janitor opened the lid of the desk, at the same time saying:

"I'd better take the teacher's things out and keep them for her until morning. What with the ink and water, everything may be spoiled."

A bright light shone in on the Monkey and the Doll when the top of the desk was opened by the janitor. Of course both the toys kept very still as soon as the janitor looked at them. This was the rule, as I have told you in the other books.

It did not take the school janitor long to cork the ink bottle and stop any more of the black fluid running out.

"Well, well!" said the janitor, looking at the ink-splashed Doll and the ink-tipped Monkey. "I'll take these two toys home and maybe my little girl can clean them. Then I'll bring them back to school to-morrow, and the teacher can give them to whoever owns them. Yes, I'll take the Monkey and Doll home to my house."

And this the janitor did. He stuffed the Monkey on a Stick, and also the Cotton Doll, into his pocket, taking care, of course, not to break them, and then, having cleaned from the room as much of the water as he could, the janitor went home.

"Look what I've brought you," he said to his little girl, as he took the Monkey and the Doll out of his pocket on reaching home.

"Oh, aren't they funny!" cried the little girl, dancing up and down. "May I have them to keep?"

"Gracious me! what is going to happen now?" thought the Monkey on a Stick.

CHAPTER IV

A QUEER RIDE

"Look out for the ink on the Doll's face," said the janitor to his little girl, as he handed her the toy. "And see, the Monkey also has ink on the end of his tail. I brought them home to you, to see if you could clean them."

"Oh, then I can't keep them!" exclaimed the little girl in a sad voice. "And they are so cute, too, even if they are covered with ink! How did it happen?"

"A water pipe burst in the school, and there was so much running around that an ink bottle in the teacher's desk got upset, I suppose, and then the ink splashed on the Monkey and the Doll," said the janitor.

"But how did they get in the teacher's desk?" the little girl wanted to know.

"I guess she must have taken them away from the children who had them out, playing with them during lesson time," answered the janitor. And he was right about that, as we know, but he was wrong about the bottle of ink.

"But perhaps you can clean them," said the janitor to his little girl. "That's why I brought the toys home to you."

"Yes, I can wash the Doll's face with soap and water," answered the little girl. "But I don't believe I can get the ink off the Monkey's tail. He's made of plush, and ink stains that very badly."

Then she got a basin of soap and water and began to wash the Doll's face. In a little while the ink spots began to fade away, for the Doll's head was of porcelain, though she was stuffed with cotton.

"It's going to leave the Doll a little darker color, though," said the little girl to her father. "I can't get her as nice and white as she was at first."

"Well, never mind, you can pretend she went to the seashore and got tanned," said the janitor, laughing. "Did you get the ink out of the Monkey's tail?" he asked.

"No, it won't come out," was the answer, and it would not. The ink on the tail of the Monkey on a Stick was there to stay, so it seemed.

"There! Just see what happened by your fooling!" said the Doll to the Monkey a little later, when they were left alone for a few minutes. "My face will always be dark, and your tail will be inky."

"I don't so much mind about my tail," answered the Monkey. "I think it will be rather stylish to have it dark and inky on the end. But I am sorry about your face. I never thought about the ink staying on or I never would have daubed you the way I did."

"Well, don't feel too bad about it," advised the Doll, with a smile. "I just happened to remember that it is stylish to be tanned. All the other dolls and toys will think I have spent a vacation at the seashore, as the janitor says. Really, after I get used to it, I shall be glad you put the ink on me."

But the Monkey still felt sorry.

That night the janitor's little girl played with the Monkey on a Stick, making him do all sorts of funny tricks. He would climb up when she pulled the string, and sometimes he would just stand up on the top of his stick, almost as straight as the Bold Tin Soldier.

Then, again, he would turn over backward and slide down head first to the bottom of the pole. Another time he would tumble forward and slide down the other way, turning somersaults on the trip.

"Oh, I just love this Monkey!" said the little girl.

In the morning the janitor took back to school in his pocket the Monkey and the Doll.

"Be sure and bring them to me again, if nobody wants them!" called the little girl, who had almost got the Doll's face clean.

"I will," her father promised.

The school was all right again the next day. The broken pipes had been mended, and the boys and girls could come back to their lessons. The teacher in the room where Herbert, Dick and their friends studied was much surprised when the janitor gave her the Doll and the Monkey, and told about finding them in her desk with an upset bottle of ink. He related how he had taken them home over -night for safe keeping.

"And so your little girl cleaned them," said the teacher. "That was very good of her, and I am going to make her happy. You may take back to her this doll, with the make-believe tanned face."

"Are you really going to give my little girl the doll?" asked the janitor.

"Yes," replied the teacher. "The little girl from whom I took the doll is not coming back to this school any more, and her mother sent word I might give the doll away. So I'll give her to your little girl."

"That is very kind of you," said the janitor. "My little girl will be happy."

The Monkey was put back in the desk until after school. Then Herbert was called up.

"Here is your Monkey on a Stick, Herbert," said the teacher. "You must not bring him to school again."

"No'm, I won't!" promised the little boy.

"I am sorry he got that blot of ink on the end of his tail," went on the teacher.

"Oh, I don't mind," said Herbert, with a smile. "He can climb his stick just the same."

And the Monkey really could. The ink on his tail didn't bother him a bit. Up and down the stick he went, when Herbert pulled the string, and even the teacher had to laugh, the Monkey was so funny.

"I'm so glad I have my Monkey back!" thought Herbert as he ran along the street.

All the other boys and girls were ahead of him, as he had been kept in a little while after school to get his toy back. All at once, as Herbert was passing a candy store, he saw, coming out of it, Dick, the boy who owned the White Rocking Horse.

"Oh, hello, Herbert!" called Dick, giving his friend a piece of candy. "So you have your Monkey back!"

"Yes," Herbert answered. "I stayed in to get him."

"I know how we can have some fun with him," went on Dick.

"How?" Herbert wanted to know.

"We can give him a ride on the back of our dog Carlo," went on Dick. "We can take the Monkey off the stick, and tie him on Carlo's back. Then Carlo will run and the Monkey will have a fine ride."

The two boys hurried down the street toward Dick's house.

"This world is full of surprises," thought the Monkey. "I wonder what my toy friends in the store would think if they knew I was going to have a ride on a dog's back. What a wonderful adventure it may be!"

The Monkey was not afraid. He was a courageous chap, almost as brave as the Bold Tin Soldier. One has to be brave to climb up and down a stick day after day, and turn somersaults from the top; I think.

"How can we make my Monkey stay on your Carlo's back?" asked Herbert, as they reached Dick's house.

"We can tie him on, same as my sister once tied her Sawdust Doll to the back of the Lamb on Wheels," Dick answered.

"And maybe, some day, we can have a little show," said Herbert.

"What kind of show?" Dick asked, as he ate the last piece of candy he had bought on his way from school, having shared some with Herbert.

"Oh, a show with my Monkey in it, and your Rocking Horse, and Arnold's Tin Soldiers, and Mirabell's Lamb and Madeline's Candy Rabbit," Herbert replied.

"Here, Carlo! Carlo!" called Dick. "Come and give Herbert's Monkey a ride on your back."

Carlo came running up, wagging his tail. He liked to play with the boys, and he did not make a bit of fuss when Dick and Herbert tied the Monkey on his back. Of course the Monkey was taken off his stick for this strange ride. He was tied on with bits of string, as the boys had plenty of this in their pockets.

"Hold still a minute, Carlo!" called Dick, for the dog was wiggling and twisting around. "Hold still and we'll soon be ready."

"How are you going to make him run, after we get the Monkey fastened on his back?" asked Herbert.

"Oh, that's easy," Dick answered. "We'll just run down the meadow toward the brook and he'll follow us all right. He'll give the Monkey a fine ride, won't you, Carlo?"

"Bow wow!" barked the dog, which, I suppose, was his way of saying: "Yes!"

"Well, I surely hope nothing serious will happen," thought the Monkey, as he found himself being tied on the dog's fuzzy back. "I have had many adventures, but never one like this. I hope nothing terrible happens!"

In another minute the boys tied the last knot. There sat the Monkey, off his stick, on Carlo's back.

"Come on, now!" cried Dick, and he and Herbert started to run.

With a bark Carlo took after them, the Monkey bobbing backward and forward on the dog's back.

"As long as they can't very well see me, I'll grab hold of the dog's hair in my hands," said the Monkey. "In that way I can hold on better. Some of the strings may break."

He clutched his hands tightly in the dog's hair. Carlo ran faster and faster after the boys.

"Don't go so quick!" begged the Monkey.

"Bow wow! I have to!" barked Carlo.

"Oh, I know something dreadful will happen!" exclaimed the Monkey. "I just know it!"

CHAPTER V

MONKEYSHINES

Over the green meadow, with the Monkey on his back, ran Carlo the dog. In front of the dog raced Herbert and Dick, now and then looking back and laughing. It was great fun for the boys to see the Monkey having a ride on the dog's back. And, to tell the truth, Carlo and the Monkey were enjoying it themselves.

"Do I hurt you, holding on this way?" asked the Monkey of Carlo, grasping tightly the dog's woolly back. "Do I pull your hair any?"

"Oh, not much," Carlo barked in answer. "I don't mind a little pull like that."

"You see I'm so afraid of falling off and breaking my tail, or something like that," went on the Monkey.

"Well, you're tied on, so I don't believe you'll fall," replied the dog. "Those boys are used to tying things. Once they tied Madeline's Candy Rabbit on the end of a kite tail, and he nearly went to the moon, I guess."

"Oh, yes, I heard about that," said the Monkey. "Only I heard it was a star, not the moon."

And then he noticed that he was tied on rather tightly, and he felt there was not much chance of his falling. So he did not hold so hard to the dog's back, and Carlo was glad of this.

Herbert and Dick, looking back to see if Carlo was running after them (which indeed he was) saw the Monkey bobbing to and fro on the dog's back.

"It looks just as if the Monkey was holding on, doesn't it?" asked Dick of his chum.

"Yes, it does," admitted Herbert. "Wouldn't it be funny if my Monkey was really alive, as your dog is, and could ride him whenever he wanted to?"

"It would be funny," said Dick. "Very funny!"

Pretty soon the boys came to a little brook that ran through the meadow. They stopped on the edge, and looked down into the water in which tiny fishes were swimming.

"Shall we jump across the brook and run in the field on the other side?" asked Dick of Herbert.

"If we do, won't Carlo jump over, too?" asked Herbert. "And if he tries to jump over, he may fall in and get all wet, and so will my Monkey."

"Carlo won't mind getting wet!" laughed Dick. "But it might not be good for your Monkey. Perhaps we'd better stay on this side of the brook, and then everything will be all right."

"I think so, too!" agreed Herbert.

So the two boys did not try to jump over the stream, but waited on the edge of it for Carlo to catch up to them. Along came the fussy little dog, barking and yelping, for he did not like to be left very far behind. And on his back, still bobbing about, was the Monkey on a Stick. No, I am wrong. The Monkey was not on his Stick just then. Herbert had taken him off to give him a ride. It was easy to take the Monkey off his Stick and put him back on.

Up ran Carlo; and as soon as he saw the brook full of water what did that little dog do but start to run right into it!

"Oh, look out! Stop him!" cried Herbert. "He'll get my Monkey all wet and spoil him!"

"Come back, Carlo! Come back!" ordered Dick, making a jump toward his pet.

But Carlo had no idea of going too deep into the brook. He just wanted to get a drink. So he waded in only a little way, stopping just before the dangling feet of the Monkey would have got wet.

"Oh, I guess he isn't going to roll in the water," said Dick. "Sometimes he does that—just rolls right over in it like a fish."

"If he did that now, with my Monkey on his back, he'd spoil him," said Herbert. "I'm glad he didn't."

Carlo lapped the cool water up with his red tongue, and then he waded out of the brook and toward the boys. He seemed to be asking them:

"What shall we do next? That was fun—giving the Monkey a ride. But what shall we do next?"

"I know what we can do," said Dick to Herbert, after they had sailed some little make-believe ships in the brook, while Carlo lay in the grass on the bank. "We can take your Monkey and my dog down the street. People will see him and laugh. Shall we do that?"

"Oh, yes. Let's do it!" exclaimed Herbert.

Once more the boys started to run across the meadow, and Carlo, seeing them go, and not wanting to be left behind, started after them with a "bow-wow." The Monkey was still on his back.

The two boys were almost across the meadow, and were thinking what fun it would be to see the dog going down the street, giving the Monkey a ride, when, all of a sudden, Carlo saw a cat.

Now you know what dogs do when they see cats. They chase them, just for fun, you understand. And this is what Carlo did—he raced after this cat as fast as he could go.

"Carlo!" chattered the Monkey.

Now, somehow or other, the strings by which the boys had fastened the Monkey on the back of the dog had become loosened. One knot after another came undone, and the Monkey felt himself slipping.

"Oh, wait a minute! Wait a minute, Carlo!" cried the Monkey, for he could talk now, being out of hearing of the boys. "Wait! Wait!" cried the Monkey. "I am falling off!"

"I can't wait!" barked Carlo. "I must get that cat!"

On he ran, faster than before. Dick and Herbert saw him, and Dick cried:

"Oh, look at my dog chasing a cat. Let's see if he gets her."

So they ran after the dog.

Faster and faster went Carlo, and the strings that held the Monkey on became looser and looser until, at last, they slipped off altogether, and down fell the Monkey into the grass.

The grass was tall and thick, and at the moment when the Monkey fell Dick and Herbert were down in a sort of little valley, and they did not see what had happened. So the Monkey fell off the dog's back before they noticed it.

As for Carlo, all he was thinking of was getting the cat. And the boys went after him.

On all sides of the Monkey was green grass, nice and soft. A little farther off were some trees. The Monkey could see them as he looked over the top of the grass.

"I wish I could climb one of those trees," said the toy Monkey half aloud. "I've been climbing up and down a stick so long that I am rather tired of it. I think I ought to climb trees."

The Monkey was beginning to feel strange. It was the first time he had ever been by himself, alone in a green field, with the warm sun shining on him.

"I feel just like doing something!" said the Monkey, speaking out loud this time, though he could see no one to whom he might talk. "I'm going to cut up! Hi yi!" he shouted. "I'm going to jump and turn somersaults and everything."

And with that he began leaping about on the soft, green grass. He jumped this way and that. He jumped forward and backward and he turned front somersaults and backward somersaults.

Then, all of a sudden, a voice called, saying:

"What in the world are you doing, my friend?"

The Monkey stopped short, and flipped his tail from side to side.

"Well, I don't see you, and I don't know who you are," he said, "but if you want to know what I'm doing, I'm cutting up Monkeyshines! That's what I'm doing! Cutting up Monkeyshines!"

CHAPTER VI

IN A CAVE

Out from under a large, green leaf, underneath which he had been sitting, crawled a long green creature. The green creature looked at the brown Monkey, who, after jumping about, sat down on a little hummock of grass to rest.

"What did you say you were doing?" asked the bug.

"Cutting up Monkeyshines," was the answer. "We Monkeys, whether we are toys or not, call our fun 'Monkeyshines,' and I thought I'd cut up a few while I was here by myself. I didn't know you minded."

"Oh, bless you, I don't mind," said the green creature. "I like to watch you. It is fun. You are quite a jumper, and I am something of a jumper myself."

"Who are you?" asked the Monkey.

"I'm a Grasshopper," was the answer. "I live here in this green meadow and sing songs all day long."

"I am glad to meet you, Mr. Grasshopper," said the Monkey. "Singing songs must be nice."

So the Monkey and the Grasshopper sat there talking together. The Monkey told the different things that had happened to him from the time he had awakened in a box on the breakfast table until he fell off Carlo's back.

"Do you have any adventures here in the meadow?" asked the chap who had been cutting up Monkeyshines.

"Oh, yes, we have had things happen here," said the Grasshopper. "Of course they are not as exciting as those you have told me about. But we rather like them. Do you want to——"

But just then something began running through the tall grass a short distance away from where the Monkey sat on a hummock. At first the Monkey thought it was Carlo, the dog, coming back, but in another moment he saw a pink nose and two long, flapping ears.

He knew then it was not Carlo, but he thought it was another friend of his, so the Monkey called:

"I say! Hold on there a minute! I want to talk to you, my friend! Wait, can't you?"

"Who is it?" asked the Grasshopper, stretching out one long hind leg. "Who do you see?"

"My friend, the Candy Rabbit," was the answer. "He just ran through the grass."

"That isn't a Candy Rabbit," said the Grasshopper.

"Who is it, then?" asked the Monkey, in surprise.

"That's Jack Hare, a real, live rabbit who lives in the meadow here," was the reply. "He wouldn't like it if you called him a Candy Rabbit."

The grass waved to and fro, and a moment later a big, white rabbit came jumping through, and sat down on his hind legs near the big leaf on which the Grasshopper was perched. The Monkey could see that this rabbit was different from the one made of candy. This bunny was larger, and his nose was not so pink. His ears, too, were bigger.

"Hello, who's your friend, Mr. Grasshopper?" asked Jack Hare.

"He is a stranger in our meadow," was the answer. "I just met him. He was cutting up some—er—polishes, I think he said."

"Shines! Shines! Monkeyshines, not polishes, though they are somewhat alike," explained the Monkey. "I cut some Monkeyshines after I fell off a dog's back."

"A dog! Good gracious! Don't tell me there's a dog around here!" exclaimed Jack Hare, looking quickly over his shoulder. "A dog will chase me as soon as he will a cat. I guess I'd better be going."

"Oh, don't be afraid," said the Monkey. "The dog I mean is Carlo. He is chasing a cat now, and so he won't come here."

The Grasshopper and the Live Rabbit sat looking at the Monkey. Soon, from under another leaf, came hopping a black bug not quite as large as the green one. The black bug wiggled her legs and chirped cheerfully:

"Well, well! Whom have we here?"

"Oh, this is Mr. Monkey Shine," said the Grasshopper. "Allow me to introduce you to Mr. Monkey Shine, Miss Cricket!" and the green creature nodded from one to the other.

"Excuse me, I am Monkey on a Stick, not Monkey Shine, though I do cut up shines once in a while," said the jolly chap who had fallen off Carlo's back. "That is my right name—Monkey on a Stick."

"I'm pleased to meet you," chirped the Cricket. "Welcome to our meadow, Monkey on a Stick."

"Thank you," replied the Monkey.

Then the Grasshopper, the Live Rabbit and the Cricket sat and looked at the Monkey, and, after a while, he cut some more Monkeyshines for them, even standing on his head and waving his tail in the air.

"I wonder if I could do that," said Jack Hare. "I'm going to try."

"Better not," warned the Monkey. "In turning over you might break off your ears."

"Oh, my ears are not made of candy. They will bend, and not break," said Jack Hare. "Here goes! I'm going to turn a somersault just as you did. Maybe I can cut some Monkeyshines, too!"

Well, the Live Rabbit tried, but I can not say that he did it very well. First he fell over to one side, and then he fell to the other side. And once he got stuck in the middle, standing on his head with his ears lying flat along the ground and his legs sticking up in the air.

"Go on over! Why don't you turn all the way over?" asked the Grasshopper.

Monkey Does Some "Monkey Shines."

"I—I can't!" answered the Live Rabbit. "I seem to be stuck half way! If one of you would be so kind as to give me a push, or a pull, I might finish my somersault. Come on, help me!"

"I'll help you," kindly said the Monkey. He took hold of the Live Rabbit's hind legs and gave him a push. Over went Jack Hare, finishing his somersault, though not doing it very well.

The Live Rabbit thanked the Monkey on a Stick for what he had done and then said:

"Since you have come to our meadow would you not like to visit my house?"

"Where do you live?" asked the Monkey.

"In a burrow, or underground house, called a cave," answered the Rabbit. "Perhaps you may not like it, but we Bunnies think it rather nice. Will you come to my cave, and visit the other Rabbits?"

"I should love to," said the Monkey. "But you see I belong to a little boy named Herbert. He got me for a birthday present, and he and Dick tied me on the dog's back. I fell off and the two boys may come back here to look for me. If I should go to your cave they might come here, and, not finding me, might think I had left them forever. I like Herbert, and as his friends have some of the other toys with whom I used to live in the store, I want to stay with him."

"That is easily managed," said the Grasshopper. "You go and visit Jack Hare's cave, Mr. Monkey. Miss Cricket and I will stay here, and if we see the boys and the dog coming back, looking for you, we'll hop over and tell you."

So it was planned that the Monkey should visit the Rabbit's cave, and if by any chance, Herbert and Dick came back, the Grasshopper and Cricket would bring word to the Monkey, who could quickly hop back.

"Come along, Mr. Monkey," called the Rabbit, and soon the two new friends were jumping through the grass together. The Monkey was off his stick, and so he could get along quite well, though not quite so fast as Jack Hare. But the Rabbit took short jumps and did not get too far ahead, waiting for the Monkey to catch up to him.

"Here we are at my cave," said Jack Hare at length, stopping in front of a hole in the ground.

"Oh, so this is where you live, is it?" asked the Monkey. He had hopped across the green meadow through the grass after his new friend.

"Yes, we'll go down in now, and meet Mrs. Hare and the children," went on the Live Rabbit. "Mind your step, and don't fall. It's rather steep until you get inside."

"And it's dark, too," said the Monkey, following the Rabbit down the hole into the ground. "How in the world do you see?"

"Oh, I forgot you aren't like us animals, and can not see quite so well in the dark," said the Live Rabbit. "Just a moment, I'll turn on the lamps."

He stopped and gave three thumps with, his feet on the earthen sides of the cave. Instantly a soft glow shone all around, and the Monkey could see very well indeed.

"Do you have electric lights?" he asked in surprise.

"No. These are lightning bugs," was the Rabbit's answer. "I keep them to make the place bright when strangers come. We Rabbits don't need light ourselves, for we can see in the dark."

"Some of the toys can, also," said the Monkey. "But I am not very good at that sort of thing yet. I like light. We had gas and electricity at the toy store."

The Monkey followed the Live Rabbit on down through the winding burrow. It twisted and turned, this way and that, now to the right and now to the left. Here and there, clinging to the earthen sides, were lightning bugs, which made the place so bright that the Monkey did not stumble once.

"But why does it twist and turn so, like a corkscrew?" the Monkey asked the Rabbit.

"We always build our burrow caves like this, to keep out dogs and other enemies," was the reply. "My real home is still a little farther on. We'll be there in a moment."

The Monkey followed on, and soon came to a place where, seated about a table made from a piece of a flat stump, were several little Rabbit children and a lady Rabbit.

"This is my family," said the Live Rabbit. "Mrs. Hare, allow me to present Mr. Monkey on a Stick, who has come to pay us a visit."

"Pleased to meet you," said Mrs. Rabbit, bowing low.

"Hi, Daddy!" called one of the little Rabbits, "where's his stick?"

And then everybody laughed.

CHAPTER VII

OUT IN THE RAIN

"Please excuse little Johnnie Hare," said Mrs. Hare to the Monkey. "He didn't mean to be impolite, asking for your stick."

"Oh, I know," said the Monkey. "He's just like all children—they just ask what they want to know about. And I suppose it does seem funny to be a Monkey on a Stick and then not have your stick with you. But I can tell you where my stick is, Johnnie," said the Monkey to the little Rabbit chap, and then he related his adventure on Carlo's back.

"Oh! Oh! Oh!" said all the other little Rabbits, opening wide their eyes when they heard this story. "Tell us another, please!"

"We are just going to have dinner," said Mrs. Hare. "Won't you sit down, Mr. Monkey on a Stick, and take something? We have some nice carrots and turnips."

"Thank you, I'll take a little," said the Monkey.

A little chair, made from a piece of wood gnawed out by Mr. Jack Hare, was brought up for the Monkey to sit on, and then the Rabbit family and the visitor gathered around the table and began eating. I can not say that the little Rabbit children ate much, for they turned around so often to look at Mr. Monkey, that, half the time, they missed putting things in their mouths and dropped them on the table.

But no one minded this, and every one laughed, so there was a most jolly good time. The lightning bugs kept on glowing, so it was not at all dark in the cave, though it would have been only for these fireflies. Mr. and Mrs. Hare had many questions to ask Mr. Monkey on a Stick about his adventures, and he told them of the Calico Clown, the Sawdust Doll and others from the toy store, including the Candy Rabbit.

"Just fancy!" exclaimed Mrs. Hare. "A Rabbit made of candy! I'm glad you're not that kind, Jack."

"So am I," said her husband. "I'd be afraid, every time I jumped, that I'd break a leg or an ear, if I were made of candy."

"Now I must show you our cave house," said Mrs. Hare, when the meal was finished. "We think it is very nice."

"I'm sure it is," returned the Monkey.

So he was taken about, and he looked at the different burrows, or rooms, in the cave house of Mr. Jack Hare. There were rooms for the children Rabbits and rooms for Mr. and Mrs. Hare. In each room were lightning bugs to give light, though as Mr. Hare said, they were needed only when company came that could not see well in the dark.

"We put out every light when Mr. Mole comes," said Mrs. Hare.

"Why is that?" asked the Monkey.

"Because he has no eyes, and doesn't need to see," was the answer. "He just feels and noses his way around. All darkness is the same to him."

"Dear me! Well, I like a little light," said the Monkey. "But I think now, since I have been here quite a while, that I had better go back. Herbert and Dick might be walking over the meadow, looking for me, for they know which way Carlo ran, with me on his back, and they often find things that are lost—those boys do."

"Oh, stay just a little longer," urged Mrs. Hare.

"And tell us another story!" begged Johnnie Hare.

"Well, I will," said the Monkey, and he did. He told about some of the funny things that had happened in the toy store—things I have told you children about in the other books. And the bunny boys and girls liked the story told by the Monkey on a Stick very much indeed.

The Monkey enjoyed himself so much in the cave house of Mr. Jack Hare that he stayed longer than he intended. It was along in the middle of the afternoon before he came out, and as the Monkey and Mr. Hare reached the outer opening of the burrow the rabbit gentleman knocked on the ground three times with his hind feet.

"What's that for?" asked the Monkey.

"To turn off the lightning bugs," was the answer. "No use burning lights when no one needs them. I'll turn them on if you call again."

"Thank you, I shall be glad to pay you another visit," said the Monkey. "But just now I feel that I must get back to where you first saw me. I want to ask the Grasshopper or Miss Cricket if they have seen the boys or the dog."

"Well, if you'll excuse me, I think I'll not go back with you," said the Rabbit. "I am not fond of dogs, and they are altogether too fond of me. Good-bye!"

Then he hopped away, waving his paw at the Monkey, and the Monkey jumped through the grass to the place where he had fallen from the dog's back.

There he found Mr. Grasshopper and Miss Cricket. They were eating some of the green things that grew all around them.

"Have you seen anything of my friends?" asked the Monkey, as he hopped up and sat on the hummock of grass where he had been resting after cutting up his Monkeyshines.

"No, neither the boys nor the dog have been here," said the Grasshopper.

"But I heard a dog barking," said Miss Cricket. "It may have been the Carlo you spoke about."

"And I heard some boys talking," went on the Grasshopper. "They may have been Dick and Herbert. But they did not come here. Why don't you jump along until you find them?"

"Yes, I suppose I could do that," agreed the Monkey. "But I'll wait a little while, and, if they don't come for me, I'll see if I can find them. As soon as I see them, though, I shall have to stop, and not move. We toys are not allowed to move or talk as long as human eyes see us."

"That's a funny rule," said Miss Cricket. "But then you are a funny fellow, Mr. Monkey on a Stick."

"If you think I'm funny, you ought to see my friend, the Calico Clown," said the Monkey. "He's full of jokes and riddles. He has a queer one about a pig making a noise under a gate."

"My goodness! why did he do that?" asked the Grasshopper.

"Do what?" inquired the Monkey.

"Why did the pig make a noise under the gate?" the Grasshopper wanted to know. "Why couldn't he stay in his pen where he belonged, or in the barnyard?"

"That's what the riddle's about, I suppose," said the Monkey. "Anyhow, none of us can answer, and the Clown's always asking it. If you want to see some one really funny, meet the Calico Clown."

After a little more talk among the three friends, the Monkey said he thought he would hop along and see if he could find the two boys or the dog.

"Aren't you afraid, if you find the dog alone, he may bite you?" asked the Grasshopper.

"Oh, my, no!" exclaimed the Monkey. "Carlo is a friend of mine. If he found me he would take me home to Herbert's house. I had even rather find him than the boys, for I can talk to the dog, and I can't talk to Dick and Herbert."

"Well, we wish you luck," chirped the Cricket, and the Grasshopper did also.

Away hopped the Monkey, making his journey through the tall grass of the green meadow. The grass was rather high, and he could not see very well. But he looked the best he could on every side, and, every now and then, he stopped to listen.

He wanted to hear the barking of Carlo or the shouts of Dick and Herbert, who, as he guessed, were, even then, looking for him. But the boys looked in the wrong place, and, as it happened, the Monkey jumped in the wrong direction.

The only creatures the Monkey met were bugs and beetles, butterflies and birds, grasshoppers and crickets in the grass. They all spoke to him kindly, and though some of them said they had seen or heard the boys and the dog, none seemed able to tell the Monkey how to find his friends.

"And it is getting late, too," said the Monkey to himself, as he looked up at the sky. "Soon the sun will set, and it will be dark. And then it will be so much the harder for me to find Dick and Herbert and Carlo, or for them to find me. Well, I suppose I must make the best of it."

He was a plucky Monkey chap, almost as adventurous as the Bold Tin Soldier, and he kept jumping on through the tall grass of the meadow. All at once, as he skipped along, being able to move quite fast now that he was off his stick, the Monkey stumbled over a stone and fell flat down.

"Ouch!" he cried, as he picked himself up. "I hope I haven't broken anything."

Very luckily he had not. He was as good as ever, except that his plush fur was rumpled a bit. But he soon brushed himself smooth again, and he was about to hop on, when, all at once, he felt a splash of water on his head.

"Dear me! is some one squirting water at me from a toy rubber ball or a water pistol?" exclaimed the Monkey.

More drops splashed down, dozens and dozens of them. Then the Monkey looked up and cried:

"Oh, it's raining! It's pouring! I'll be soaking wet! I'll be drowned out in the rain without an umbrella or rubbers! Oh, my!"

And the rain came down harder and harder and harder.

CHAPTER VIII

HERBERT FINDS THE MONKEY

Poor Monkey on a Stick! Oh, I forgot! He wasn't on a stick now, was he? Herbert had the stick, and it was just as well he had, for the Monkey, being rid of it, could hop around better.

"And I need to hop around a lot, to keep out of the wet," said the Monkey to himself, after he had come from the Rabbit's cave and had been caught in the rain.

Harder and harder the big drops came pelting down. At first the Monkey tried to keep dry by crawling under the grass. But, thick and tall as it was, it was not like an umbrella, and the drops came through. Soon the Monkey was very wet.

"I know I'll catch cold!" he said sorrowfully. "I'll get the snuffles! I'm not used to being soaked like this."

And, truly, he was not. Since he had been made at the workshop of Santa Claus, the Monkey had never been out in a rain storm. He had always been either in the toy factory, the department store, or in some house, and when he was taken from one place to another he was always well wrapped up, so it did not matter whether there was snow or rain.

But now it was different. The Monkey was getting wetter and wetter each minute.

"It's the first time I've been in so much water since the janitor's little girl tried to wash the ink spot off the end of my tail," the Monkey said.

Just then he heard a voice calling:

"Come over here, Mr. Monkey! Over this way, and you can stand under this big leaf, which is like an umbrella!"

"Hello! Who are you?" asked the Monkey, looking around, but seeing no one. By this time he had crossed the green meadow and was near a little clump of trees.

"I am Jack in the Pulpit," was the answer. "I live on the edge of the woods. There are big fern leaves here under which you can be safe from the rain. Hop over!"

So the Monkey hopped through the wet grass until he came close to the trees in the woods. Then the voice called again:

"Straight ahead now, and you'll see me!"

The Monkey looked, and saw a queer little thin green chap, standing up in the middle of a sort of brown, striped leaf that curled over his head, just as in some churches the pulpit curls down over the preacher's head.

"Who did you say you were?" asked the Monkey.

"I am Jack in the Pulpit," was the answer. "Some folks call me a plant, and others a flower. They don't know I am really alive, and can come to life as you toys do. I saw you getting wet, so I called to you. Get under one of these big, broad fern leaves, and it will keep the rain off as well as an umbrella."

Jack in the Pulpit nodded toward a big fern leaf near where he himself was growing, and in an instant the Monkey had crawled under this shelter. Truly enough it kept off the rain, the drops pattering down on the leaf over the Monkey's head as they used to patter on the roof of the toy store. No longer was he out in the rain.

"Thank you for telling me how to keep out of the wet," said the Monkey to Jack in the Pulpit.

"Oh, you are very welcome," was the answer. "And now please tell me about yourself and whether you have had any adventures. I love to hear about adventures."

So the Monkey told all about himself, even down to the time when he fell off Carlo's back and visited the cave of Jack Hare.

"And I suppose Herbert is looking for me now," said the Monkey.

"Oh, I hardly think he would be looking for you in all this rain," said Jack in the Pulpit. "Besides it will soon be night. You had better make up your mind to stay here until morning. Then the sun will be shining and you can hop back to the place where you fell off the dog's back. Then Herbert and Dick may come along and find you."

"That's what I'll do," said the Monkey.

Just as the Jack had said it would, it soon became dark, and it kept on raining. But the Monkey curled up under the big fern leaf, where it was nice and dry. Soon the Monkey began to feel warm and sleepy, and, before he knew it, he was fast asleep.

In the morning the rain had stopped. The sun came out bright and warm and dried up the damp grass. Jack in the Pulpit awoke, and, looking over toward the Monkey, fast asleep under the broad leaf, called:

"Hi, there, Mr. Monkey! It's morning! Now maybe you can find Herbert, or he can find you!"

"Dear me! Morning so soon?" exclaimed the Monkey, stretching out his legs. "I must have slept very soundly."

"Did you dream any?" asked the Jack.

"Not that I remember," was the answer. "But I am glad the rain has stopped. Now I'll hop over the meadow, back to the place where I fell off Carlo's back, and I'll wait there until Herbert comes for me, as I am sure he will."

"I shall be sorry to see you go," said Jack, "but I suppose it has to be. If you ever get back this way again, stop and see me."

The Monkey said he would and then, smoothing down his plush, he sat out in the sun awhile to get a little dryer and warmer. He looked at the end of his tail.

"The ink is almost washed off," he said. "I am glad of that."

Then he began to hop across the field, making his way through the tall grass. He thought he would know it when he came to the place where the string had come loose, and where he had fallen from Carlo's back, but the grass looked so much alike all over that the Monkey was beginning to think he might be lost in it.

All at once, however, he heard a voice saying:

"Well, you've come back, have you?"

The Monkey looked around, and there sat his friend Mr. Grasshopper, and near him was Miss Cricket.

"Oh, I'm so glad to see you!" cried the Monkey. "I was looking for the place I first met you—the place where I fell off the dog's back."

"It is right here," said the Grasshopper. "This is where I first noticed you. And there is the hummock of grass you sat on."

Then the Monkey knew he was back at the place he wished to reach. He sat down and talked with the Grasshopper and the Cricket, telling them of his visit to Jack Hare's cave, and also how he had slept all night under a leaf near Jack in the Pulpit.

"Hark!" suddenly called the Grasshopper.

"What's the matter?" asked the Monkey.

"I think you are going to get your wish," was the Grasshopper's answer. "I hear boys talking and a dog barking. We had better be going, Miss Cricket. Good-bye, Mr. Monkey on a Stick!"

"Good-bye," called the Cricket.

With that they hopped away. The Monkey listened, and, surely enough, he heard the barking of a dog and the talking of two boys.

"It was right about here he must have fallen off," said one boy.

"It might have been farther on," said another boy.

And just then the grass began to wave from side to side, and through it came bursting Carlo, the little dog! At once he saw the Monkey.

"Bow wow! Oh, here you are!" barked Carlo. "I thought I should find you."

"I'm glad you did," said the Monkey. Then the two friends had no further chance to talk, for Dick and his chum came running along when they heard the dog bark.

"Oh, here he is!" cried Herbert. "I've found my lost Monkey. Now I'm going to put him back on his stick!"

CHAPTER IX

MONKEY IN A TENT

Herbert and Dick, with Carlo the dog, had searched through the meadow all the afternoon, to find the Monkey, but they did not find him. At night the two boys had gone to their homes, and Herbert felt sad at losing his toy.

"Never mind," said Madeline, as she let Herbert hold her Candy Rabbit, "tomorrow I'll help you look for your Monkey. Maybe he's hiding down in the tall grass, as Dorothy's Sawdust Doll once did."

"Maybe," said Herbert hopefully. But still he felt sad.

The next day he and Dick and Carlo again went to the meadow. They looked all around, and at last they found the Monkey, as I have told you.

Of course neither of the boys knew what an adventure the Monkey had had, nor how he had gone to visit Jack Hare in the cave, and had seen the little Rabbits. Nor did they know how he had become dried out by sleeping under the fern leaf.

"Well, now we'll have some fun, as long as I have my Monkey back," said Herbert, and he and Dick, followed by the dog, went back across the meadow.

"What are you going to do?" asked Dick.

"Put up a tent and have a show," Herbert answered. "You can bring your White Rocking Horse, and Arnold can bring his Bold Tin Soldier. If Dorothy wants to, she can bring her Sawdust Doll, Mirabell can bring her Lamb of Wheels, and my sister Madeline can bring her Candy Rabbit."

"That'll be a fine show!" cried Dick.

The two little boys hurried back to Herbert's house, and told his mother what they were going to do. Herbert showed his mother the Monkey he had found in the meadow, and Dick hurried over to his house to get his Rocking Horse, and to tell his sister about the show.

"What can I make a tent of?" asked Herbert.

"Oh, I think I can let you take some old sheets," said his mother, "and you can hang them over the clothesline in the yard. That will make a nice little tent for your show."

"Yes, that will be fine," said Herbert. "Thank you, Mother."

He carried his Monkey into the house and put him on a table, where Madeline was sitting, playing with her Candy Rabbit.

"Watch my Monkey so he doesn't jump away, will you, please?" asked Herbert of his sister, laughing and pretending his toy was alive.

"What are you going to do?" asked Madeline.

"Make a tent to have a show," answered her brother.

"Oh, let me help!" she cried, and she set her Candy Rabbit down on the table near the Monkey and ran out with Herbert. Mother gave the children the sheet, and in a little while the sheet tent was being put up in the yard over the clothesline.

Monkey Thanks Jack in the Pulpit.

As soon as the Candy Rabbit and Monkey found themselves alone they looked at one another and began to talk, as they were allowed to do.

"Where in the world have you been?" asked the Candy Rabbit.

"You may well ask that," replied the Monkey. "I have had so many adventures, and I met some friends of yours."

"Friends of mine?" repeated the Candy Rabbit. "Do you mean the Lamb on Wheels or the Bold Tin Soldier?"

"Neither one. I mean Live Rabbits," answered the Monkey. Then he told of going to the cave of Jack Hare and of being caught in the rain storm.

"Oh, what wonderful adventures!" exclaimed the Candy Rabbit.

"What happened to you while I was away?" asked the Monkey.

"Oh, many things," answered the Candy Rabbit. "Once Madeline left me alone, and the cat came in and began to lick the sugar off my pink nose. Another time a little mouse came out of a hole in the closet where I am kept at night, and nibbled a few crumbs of sweetness off the end of my stubby tail."

"Gracious!" cried the Monkey. "Weren't you scared?"

"A little," answered the Rabbit. "But I jumped to one side, and when Madeline opened the closet door the mouse ran away."

All the while the Monkey and Candy Rabbit were talking, Herbert, Dick and Arnold, with Madeline, Dorothy and Mirabell to help, were putting up the sheet tent in Herbert's yard. The clothesline was pulled tight between two posts and the sheets put over the line. The edges were fastened to the ground with wooden rings, and then some pieces of cloth were pinned to the back of the sheet to close that end. It took two or three days to make the tent, but at last it was finished.

"We'll leave one end open for the front door," said Herbert.

"But if we do that everybody can look in and see our show for nothing," objected Dick. "That isn't right. They ought to give one pin, or two pins, to come to see our show."

"We can pin some pieces of cloth at the front end of the tent," suggested Mirabell. "I have an old shawl over at my house that Mother lets me spread on the grass when I play with my Lamb on Wheels. I'll get that to close the front of the tent."

The old shawl was just what was needed to make a front "door" for the show tent, and soon it was pinned in place. Some old boxes were found by Patrick, the kind gardener, and these were to be used for seats.

"Now we'd better all go and get our things that are going to be in the show," said Herbert. "I'll bring out my Monkey."

"And I'll get my Candy Rabbit," offered Madeline.

"I'll have to have somebody help me carry over my Tin Soldier Captain and all the men," said Arnold. "I don't want to drop any of 'em."

"I'll help you, as soon as I bring out my Monkey," offered Herbert.

"And I'd like somebody to help me carry over my Lamb," said Mirabell.

"I'll help you," said Dick. "I'll bring over my White Rocking Horse and your Lamb, Mirabell."

So, as it happened, Herbert's Monkey and Madeline's Candy Rabbit were the first of the toy friends to be brought into the tent. The Monkey was on his stick, as Herbert was going to make him do tricks by climbing up to the top of it, and turning somersaults, as it was intended for the Monkey to do.

"Do you think my Rabbit and your Monkey will be all right if we leave them here alone in the tent?" asked Madeline, as the toys were put down on one of the boxes, and she and her brother started to help the other children carry in their things.

"Oh yes, they'll be all right," said Herbert.

But he and Madeline had not been very long away, and the Monkey and Candy Rabbit had not been very long alone in the tent, before something happened.

All at once, just as the Monkey was thinking of asking the Candy Rabbit what tricks that sweet chap was going to do in the show, a loud noise was heard in the tent.

"Baa-a-a-a-!" was what the Rabbit and the Monkey heard.

"Was that you?" asked the Monkey of the Rabbit.

"I was just going to ask if you had called," said the Rabbit.

"Baa-a-a-a!" came again.

"It sounds like the Lamb on Wheels," said the Candy Rabbit.

"Oh, it can't be," said the Monkey. "She'd come in to see us. Who do you suppose it is?"

"Baa-a-a-a!" sounded again, and then a funny black nose, followed by a head with curving horns on it, was thrust into the tent.

"This isn't the Lamb!" cried the Monkey.

"Indeed I'm not a Lamb!" was the answer. "I'm a Billy Goat! Baa-a! Baa-a-a-a! What's going on here?" he bleated.

"We're going to have a show," said the Monkey. "I am going to be in it, and so is the Candy Rabbit."

"Oh, no, the Candy Rabbit isn't!" said the Goat. "He isn't going to be in the show. He's going to be in me, for I am going to eat him! I am very fond of candy, and I've been looking for some for a long time. I wondered what was in this tent, and now I know. I saw it from over in the vacant lots where I live. Then I came over to peep in, when I saw that the boys and girls had gone. Yes, indeed! I like sugar, and I'm going to eat the Candy Rabbit!"

The bad Goat, with his sharp horns, walked into the tent and over toward the box on which the Candy Rabbit sat near the Monkey on a Stick.

"Oh, yum-yum! How I love candy!" bleated the goat, wiggling his whiskers and smacking his lips. "How I love sugar! I'm going to nibble some sweetness off the ears of the Candy Rabbit."

"Oh, no you're not!" suddenly cried the Monkey.

"Why not? Who will stop me?" asked the bad Goat, stamping his foot.

"I will!" cried the brave Monkey on a Stick. "Here! You get out of this tent!" and the Monkey stood straight up on his stick and looked with both eyes at the goat.

Monkey Protects Candy Rabbit.

CHAPTER X

MONKEY IN A SHOW

The bad Goat walked closer and closer to the Candy Rabbit. And that poor Bunny toy was so frightened that he did not think of jumping out of the way.

"I'm going to get sweetness off your ears," said the Goat, teasing.

"Oh, if you bite my ears I can't be in the show!" said the poor Rabbit.

The Monkey climbed higher and higher on his stick, after he had said he would stop the Goat from eating the Candy Rabbit. And now, just as the Goat was going to take the Bunny up from the box, the Monkey suddenly gave a jump! Oh, such a jump!

Off his stick he jumped, and he landed right on the Goat's back. With his hands the Monkey began to pull the Goat's hair.

He even reached around and pulled the Goat's whiskers, the Monkey did.

"Baa-a-a-a-a!" bleated the Goat. "Stop, Monkey! You're hurting me! You're pulling my hair!"

"Then get out of this tent and leave the Candy Rabbit alone!" shouted the Monkey.

"No! I want sweet stuff!" bleated the bad Goat.

Then the Monkey jumped off the Goat's back, and, catching up the stick, on which he climbed to the top when the string was pulled, the Monkey began hitting the Goat over the nose with it.

"Oh, my nose! My soft and tender nose!" bleated the Goat, as he ran out of the tent.

"Thank you, so much, for saving me," said the Rabbit to the Monkey, as the likely chap climbed back on his stick.

"I am very glad I could help you," said the Monkey. "I guess that Goat won't come back in a hurry!"

And as the Groat ran out of the tent, the children, bringing up their other toys to have the show, saw him.

"Oh, look at the big sheep!" cried Madeline.

"That isn't a sheep, it's a goat," said her brother.

"Oh, maybe he ate my Candy Rabbit!" cried the little girl. "I must go and look."

She and the other children hurried into the tent. There were the Monkey and the Rabbit safe together. But the children did not know what a narrow escape the Rabbit had had.

By this time Arnold, with the help of the other boys, had brought over his Bold Tin Soldier and the other men in the army company; Dick had brought his White Rocking Horse; and Dorothy's Sawdust Doll and Mirabell's Lamb on Wheels were also in the tent. Of course Herbert's Monkey and Madeline's Candy Rabbit were the first to be in the show.

"Now the performance is going to start!" cried Herbert, when the brothers and sisters were seated on the benches, which were made from the boxes Patrick, the gardener, had given Dick. "The show is going to start! All ready!"

Besides the six children mentioned there were others who lived on the same street with these six friends. These children had all come to the show. The boys and girls brought two pins to get in. Those who brought toy animals to act in the show did not have to bring any pins to come in.

"The first act in the show!" called Herbert, who was the ringmaster, "will be Mr. Dick riding on his White Rocking Horse! Ladies and Gentlemen, see Mr. Dick!"

"Hurray! Hurray! Hurray!" cried the children, clapping their hands.

Dick drew his horse out into the middle of the tent. Of course if the Rocking Horse had been there alone he could have trotted out by himself. But, as it was, Dick had to drag him.

Then Dick climbed on the back of his white steed, took hold of the reins, and cried: "Gid-dap!"

Back and forth rocked Dick on his Horse, and, as I have told you in the book about this toy, the Horse could move along whenever any one was on his back. He moved just as a rocking chair moves.

Across the middle of the tent rode Dick on his Rocking Horse. The little chap pretended he was a cowboy, and swung his cap around his head, and he even made believe lasso wild bulls with a piece of clothesline.

"Bang! Bang!" cried Dick, shooting make-believe pistols the way real cowboys do.

"Hurray! Hurray! Hurray!" cried all the children, for they liked to see Dick ride the White Rocking Horse.

"What's next, Herbert?" asked Madeline.

"Hush, you mustn't talk in the show," cautioned her brother. "The ringmaster is the only one who can talk, and I'm him. The next part of the show is the dance of the Sawdust Doll."

This was Dorothy's chance, and she came out with her toy. And then and there the Sawdust Doll did a funny little dance while Mirabell played on a mouth organ. Of course Dorothy had to hold the Doll and dance around with her, but it was as good as if the Doll had done it herself, and the boys and girls clapped their hands.

"Isn't this a wonderful show?" whispered the Sawdust Doll to the Monkey, when she had a chance, as the children crowded down to one end of the tent to get some cookies Herbert's mother brought out to them.

"Yes, you did your part very well," whispered back the Monkey. "Do you think I shall get a chance to do any of my tricks?"

"Oh, yes," answered the Doll. "I'm sure you're going to be the best part of the show."

When the cookies were eaten, Herbert again took the part of ringmaster.

"The next thing in the show will be a fight with the Tin Soldiers," said Herbert. "Mr. Dick will take half of them and Mr. Arnold will take the other half, and there will be a battle right here in the tent."

Dick and Arnold divided the Tin Soldiers between them, and set them in two armies on one of the big box tops. Then the tin fighters were moved backward and forward, just as in real battle.

"Bang! Bang!" Arnold would shout. "Bang! Bang!" Dick would answer, and so the make-believe guns were fired. The Bold Tin Soldier Captain was moved to and fro, and so were the privates, the Corporal and the Sergeant.

"Now the fight is over," said Herbert, after a while. "We'll make believe both sides won, 'cause it will be nicer that way. And you can take the soldiers away, Arnold, 'cause next is going to be a race between the Candy Rabbit and the Lamb on Wheels."

"Oh, my Rabbit can't race with the Lamb!" objected Madeline. "The Lamb is too big."

"Yes, I guess that's so," admitted her brother. "Well, then the next part of the show," he cried in a loud voice, "will be when the Candy Rabbit rides around the ring on the back of the Lamb on Wheels."

"Oh, that will be nice," said Mirabell, blowing a kiss to her woolly Lamb.

The two girls left their seats and took their places in the middle of the tent. Mirabell tied a string to her Lamb and then Madeline took her Candy Rabbit and held him on the fleecy back of the Lamb.

Around and around the little grass ring in the tent rode the Candy Rabbit on the back of the Lamb, and the boys and girls thought it was a very nice part of the show. One of the Lamb's wheels squeaked a little where she had caught rheumatism after her ride down the brook.

"And now we come to the last act!" said Herbert. "This will be some tricks by my Monkey on a Stick."

"I'm glad my chance has come at last," thought the Monkey to himself. "I must do my best!"

The Monkey had got back on his stick himself after he had driven the Goat out of the tent, and now the funny chap was all ready to do whatever Herbert wanted.

"The first trick," said the little boy ringmaster, "will be turning a front somersault!"

He pulled the string, up the stick went the Monkey, and then and there, before the crowd of boys and girls in the tent, the lively fellow turned a somersault head over tail.

"Hurray! Hurray!" cried Dick and the others, clapping their hands.

"The next trick," went on Herbert, "will be when my Monkey turns a back somersault."

Once more the string was pulled. Up the stick shinned the Monkey, and, when he reached the top, he turned a back somersault. Of course this was harder than a front one, and the boys and girls clapped all the more.

"And now, Ladies and Gentlemen!" cried Herbert, just like a real ringmaster in a real circus, "the next trick will be when my Monkey does a flip-flap-flop!"

And, indeed, that was a very hard trick to do. But the Monkey did it when Herbert pulled the string, and all the boys and girls said it was fine, and that the show was one grand affair.

The Monkey did several other tricks, and then Herbert's mother, outside the tent, called, just like a circus vendor:

"Here's your pink lemonade! Here's your pink lemonade!"

And, as true as I'm telling you, she had made a big pitcher of sweet lemonade for the children, and had colored it pink with strawberry juice.

"Oh! Ah! Um!" said the boys and girls, and, really, I think the lemonade was almost as good a part of the show as the tricks of the Monkey, the fight of the Tin Soldiers, or the dance of the Sawdust Doll.

"Well, the show is over. I wonder what will happen next," said the Lamb on Wheels to the Bold Tin Captain.

"Maybe the children will have another," said the Monkey. "But, while we have the chance, I would like to talk to my friends the Sawdust Doll, the Bold Tin Soldier, the White Rocking Horse, and all the others."

And so the toys talked among themselves, and told of their different adventures, just as I have told you in the different books. And they all said the Monkey was very brave to have driven away the bad Goat as he had done.

"I'd like to know what the Calico Clown is doing all this time, since we came away from the toy store," said the Monkey, after a while.

"So would I," put in the Sawdust Doll. "I wonder if anything has happened to him."

And as perhaps you children are wondering the same thing, I have decided to make the next book about that funny chap.

The volume will be called "The Story of a Calico Clown." He had many wonderful adventures to tell about.

As for the Sawdust Doll, the Lamb on Wheels, the White Rocking Horse, the Candy Rabbit, the Bold Tin Soldier and the Monkey on a Stick, why, they had some strange adventures, too, and they took part in another show. But this is all I have to tell you just now about the Monkey on a Stick, except to say that he lived for many years with Herbert and Madeline, and had many happy times.

THE END